HOUGHTON MIFFLIN

Reading

We're a Family

 HOUGHTON MIFFLIN   BOSTON

Printed in China

ISBN - 13: 978-0-618-16189-8

ISBN - 10: 0-618-16189-9

14 15 16 17 18 19-SDP-08

Design, Art Management, and Page Production: Studio Goodwin Sturges

Contents

The Birthday Party

by Susan Gorman-Howe
illustrated by Grace Lin

4

Baby Bear's Family

by Susan Gorman-Howe
illustrated by Angela Jarecki

Cat's Surprise

by Susan Gorman-Howe
illustrated by Valeri Gorbachev

19

23